THE
NOTEBOOK OF
DOOM

MARCH OF THE VANDERPANTS

by Troy Cummings

BRANCHES

SCHOLASTIC INC.

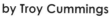

TABLE OF CONTENTS

To my pals at the Putnam County Public Library.

Thank you, Katie Carella and Kay Petronio, for all your help getting the story, pictures, and design just right—especially fitting the word "Vanderpants" 70 times.

Copyright © 2017 by Troy Cummings

All rights reserved. Published by Scholastic Inc., *Publishers since 1920.* SCHOLASTIC, BRANCHES, and associated logos are trademarks and/or registered trademarks of Scholastic Inc.

The publisher does not have any control over and does not assume any responsibility for author or third-party websites or their content.

Library of Congress Cataloging-in-Publication Data

Names: Cummings, Troy, author. | Cummings, Troy.
Notebook of doom; bk. 12.Title: March of the Vanderpants / by Troy Cummings.
Description: New York, NY : Branches/Scholastic Inc., 2017. | Series: The Notebook of Doom; 12
Summary: The Notebook of Doom is missing and Alexander and his fellow monster hunters, Rip and Nikki, are convinced that the boss-monster has it; but is that monster the mysterious Principal Vanderpants, who is certainly behaving oddly, or someone else? They need to figure that out quickly because a mistake could have deadly consequences for Stermont Elementary.
Identifiers: LCCN 2016051617 | ISBN 9781338034523 (pbk.) | ISBN 9781338034530 (hardcover)
Subjects: LCSH: Monsters—Juvenile fiction. | Elementary schools—Juvenile fiction. | School principals—Juvenile fiction. | Identity (Psychology)—Juvenile fiction. | Secrecy—Juvenile fiction. | Horror tales. | CYAC: Monsters—Fiction. | Schools—Fiction. | School principals—Fiction. | Identity—Fiction. | Secrets—Fiction. | Horror stories. | LCGFT: Horror fiction.
Classification: LCC PZ7.C91494 Mar 2017 | DDC 813.6 [Fic]-dc23 LC record available at https://lccn.loc.gov/2016051617

10 9 8 7 6 5 4 3 2 1   17 18 19 20 21

Printed in China   38
First edition, July 2017

Edited by Katie Carella
Book design by Liz Frances

CHAPTER 1

BOOK CLUB

Alexander had just gobbled up an entire bowl of Stanley Flakes when his dad shuffled into the kitchen.

"Morning, Al," said his dad, with a big yawn. "You're up early."

"I have to go to a meeting before school," said Alexander.

"I'm glad you're involved in activities outside of class!" his dad said. "Is it the chess team? Or a writing group? Or a book club?"

Alexander grabbed his backpack. "It's, uh, sort of like a book club. Just me, Rip, and Nikki.

"Neat!" said his dad. "Have fun!"

Alexander dashed out the door and into the woods behind his house.

He did have a club meeting, but this club only cared about *one* book: an old notebook full of information about monsters.

S.S.M.P. =
(Super Secret Monster Patrol!)

CREEPY SKULL!

Full of monster drawings!

The club was called the Super Secret Monster Patrol, a group of monster-fighting grade schoolers. Alexander had become leader of the S.S.M.P. shortly after moving to Stermont.

Alexander soon arrived at a broken-down caboose — the club's headquarters. The other two members, Rip and Nikki, were waiting inside. They were his two best friends, and they were both monsters.

3

"Hey, Salamander!" said Rip. Salamander was Alexander's nickname.

"How are you feeling, Rip?" Alexander asked.

"Fine," said Rip. "I haven't turned into a monster lately, if that's what you're asking."

"He's his ugly old self!" added Nikki.

"Ugly?!" said Rip. "You're just jealous because jampires aren't as awesome as Rip-monsters."

"Ha!" said Nikki. "Jampires can see in the dark! What can *you* do, besides smash stuff?"

"Don't argue, guys!" said Alexander. "You're both good monsters."

"Well, I *was* a monster," said Rip. "It hasn't happened again since I ate those cupcakes."

"So you think it's just cupcakes that make you transform?" asked Nikki.

"I'm not sure," said Rip. "Maybe it's anything sweet."

"Let's do a test," said Alexander. He pulled out a granola bar. "Here, nibble one chocolate chip off the corner."

Rip swallowed the chip.

Nothing happened. But then —

"Your ears are blue!" said Nikki.

Rip looked at his reflection. A few seconds later, his ears faded back to normal.

"Hmm . . ." said Rip. I guess anything sweet makes — ack!" He brushed his pants. "Ants!"

"Relax, Rip," said Nikki. "They're just ants. I bet they're getting in through the hole in the wall."

"We'll deal with that later," said Alexander. "We have to start our S.S.M.P. meeting."

"Right," said Rip, brushing away another ant. "So what's our super secret plan to get back the notebook?"

"Well, we know the boss-monster stole it," said Alexander.

"And that monster is probably our principal," added Nikki.

"What do you mean, 'probably'?" Rip yelled. "Vanderpants is definitely the boss-monster! She's mean, and she always seems to be around whenever monsters attack . . ."

"Good point," said Alexander. "And she keeps sneaking into this weird UPSTAIRS BASEMENT at school."

"She's up to *something* for sure!" said Nikki.

"I agree. But we don't have any real proof," said Alexander. "Just this list I grabbed from her desk." He took a bluish-green folder from his backpack.

"Everyone on that list is a monster," said Rip. "Monsters that *she* hired — because she's the boss! How much more proof do you need?"

"Maybe you're right," said Alexander. "I'll spy on her today and see what I can find. I'll start by sneaking this folder back onto her desk before she realizes I took the wrong one."

"Good luck!" said Nikki.

"See you at lunch, weenie!" said Rip.

CHAPTER 2 NOODLING AROUND

Alexander stepped into the empty lobby of Stermont Elementary.

It's weird to be early, for once, he thought. He took the escalator to the second floor, where he noticed someone moving in the distance. Two someones.

MR. HOARSELY
School secretary, janitor, nurse, bus driver, and gym teacher
Former S.S.M.P. member, and a HUGE fraidy-cat
Only grown-up who can see monsters?

MS. VANDERPANTS
Principal by day...
Boss-monster by night?
Alexander's teacher (one-on-one!)

Good, Alexander thought. *Ms. Vanderpants is not in her office!*

Alexander crouched low on the escalator to the next floor. Then he ran up the rest of the escalators — all the way to floor thirteen.

He jogged down the hallway, pausing at a heavy stone door.

There's that scratching sound again! he thought. *What is Ms. Vanderpants hiding in there?* He ran down the hall to the principal's office, which was also his classroom.

He stepped inside. Nothing seemed out of place. There was still a greenish-blue folder sitting on her desk.

Perfect! he thought. *Maybe she hasn't noticed I took the wrong folder!*

Bluish-green folder: Principal Vanderpants's list

Greenish-blue folder: Alexander's homework

Alexander switched the folders and looked back at the door. No sign of his principal.

Spy time! he thought. He glanced around the room.

Books

Big fancy desk

Potted cactus

Weird white bucket

File cabinet

Silver bell

The file cabinet in the corner, thought Alexander. *It is probably full of secrets!*

He checked over his shoulder, took a breath, and then tugged on a drawer. KER-CLICK. It was unlocked.

But there were no files inside. Instead, the drawer was filled with long flat boxes. Alexander picked one up.

"Spaghetti?" he said, in a half whisper.

He tried the other drawers. The whole cabinet was full of uncooked spaghetti.

Alexander shook a box. He opened it and gave it a sniff.

"Good morning, Alexander," said a voice from the doorway.

"Ack!" Alexander jumped.

"If you snoop around, you may not be happy with what you find," Ms. Vanderpants said with a frown. "Now clean up so we can get to work."

"Um, Ms. Vanderpants?" he asked. "Why do you have all this spaghetti?"

Ms. Vanderpants looked at Alexander over the top of her glasses. "It's for a special project I've been cooking up." She glanced down at the greenish-blue folder near Alexander's feet. "I'm glad to see you remembered your homework."

"Actually —" Alexander began.

Ms. Vanderpants flipped through the folder. "Is this a joke, Mr. Bopp? You didn't complete one problem!"

Alexander wanted to say "sorry I didn't do my homework, but I was busy saving Stermont from a monster attack that YOU set up!" But instead he just mumbled, "Sorry."

"Alexander," she said. "I chose you for this one-on-one class for a reason. I'm counting on you to finish your work, so I can give you . . . extra challenges. Do you understand?"

"Uh, yeah," Alexander said as he sat down.

Actually, no, he thought.

"Very well," said Ms. Vanderpants. "Finish your homework this morning. Then, after lunch, come straight back here to do all of today's classwork. No recess."

Alexander's eyebrows and lips tightened into stiff, straight lines, like sticks of uncooked spaghetti.

3 BUG IN THE BAG

Alexander watched his principal all morning. She signed papers and made phone calls, but she didn't do anything strange or monster-y.

Finally, it was time for lunch. Alexander dashed down to the cafeteria.

"Hi, Salamander!"

A girl was waving him over to the lunch line. A girl with a bunny backpack.

"Dottie — hey!" said Alexander. He ran up to her.

"Hope you like pork," said Dottie. She pointed to the menu.

TODAY'S MENU

- Monday: Pulled pork
- Tuesday: Shaved pork
- Wednesday: Shredded pork
- Thursday: Jerk pork
- Friday: Tuna (Pork needed a day off.)

Alexander smiled at Dottie, although he felt a tiny bit sad. She used to be a member of the S.S.M.P. but had recently left the group.

"So, um," Alexander said. He looked up at the shiny decorations. "What are all these stars and stuff for?"

"Don't you know? Today's our ninety-eighth day of school!" said Dottie. "In two days, the whole school's having a 100th Day party."

"Cool," said Alexander. He didn't say anything as they moved through the line. But by the time they got their milks, he spoke up. "Would you like to sit with me and Rip and Nikki?"

"Thanks, but I can't!" said Dottie. "Playing monsters with you guys was fun, but now I'm playing superheroes with kids from my class. Have a good lunch!"

Dottie hopped away. Alexander sighed, then headed to Rip and Nikki's table.

"What's up, Salamander?" asked Nikki.

"I just saw Dottie," said Alexander. "It's so weird how she dropped out of the S.S.M.P., right in the middle of her birthday party."

"It's too bad," said Rip with his mouth full. "She was one heck of a monster fighter! She —" Rip paused, and cocked his head to the side. "Did you hear that?"

"Hear what?" asked Alexander. He looked at Nikki, who shrugged.

"A clicking sound," said Rip. "Like tap shoes." He started chewing again. "Oh well, it stopped. I guess — HEY!"

Rip picked up his lunch sack. "Another ant?! Stay away from my raisins!" He brushed the ant away. "It must've hitched a ride on my pants from the caboose this morning."

"Or maybe Mr. Plunkett's class is making ant farms!" said Nikki, smiling.

"Ms. Vanderpants would never let him do that activity again!" said Alexander. "Remember how she freaked out about all those ants?"

"Speaking of our freaked-out principal, how was she this morning?" asked Nikki. "Were you able to switch folders before she got there?"

"Yeah," said Alexander. "And I snooped around a bit. I found a file cabinet full of spaghetti."

"Weird!" said Nikki. She ate a spoonful of BBQ sauce.

"She also said something odd about giving me extra challenges, whatever that means," said Alexander.

The recess bell rang.

"Let's go, weenie!" said Rip.

Alexander sighed. "Go on without me," he said. "I have to do make-up work. See you after school."

4 FULL STEAM AHEAD

FLOOR
13

A lexander saw a rain cloud in the thirteenth floor hallway.

Actually, it wasn't a rain cloud. It was steam. Principal Vanderpants was chugging down the hallway, lugging her strange white bucket.

Alexander followed her. She stopped in front of the UPSTAIRS BASEMENT. Her bucket sloshed, and something flew out, landing on the carpet.

Spaghetti?! thought Alexander.

Ms. Vanderpants unlocked the stone door and slowly opened it. She hauled in her bucket and pulled the door shut behind her.

Alexander picked up the wet noodle.

Why is she bringing spaghetti in there? he wondered.

SCRITCH-SCRITCH! Alexander heard more loud scraping noises from inside, and then quick footsteps. TUP-TUP-TUP!

She's coming! thought Alexander. He tossed the noodle aside and ran to her office. He pretended to study his spelling words.

A moment later, Ms. Vanderpants came in. She placed her empty bucket in the corner, wiped her brow, and picked up a rolled-up poster.

"All right, Alexander," she said. "It's time I let you in on a secret."

She handed the poster to Alexander.

He sat up in his seat. *Is this going to tell me what's inside the* UPSTAIRS BASEMENT? he wondered. *Or is it her master plan for destroying the S.S.M.P. once and for all?*

Alexander's hands were shaking as he unrolled the poster.

It wasn't a master plan. It was a picture of a grinning steam shovel.

"Stanley?" said Alexander.

"Yes," said Ms. Vanderpants. "So you're already familiar with Stanley the Steam Shovel?"

"Yeah," said Alexander. "I liked the cartoons when I was little. And my dad keeps buying me the books."

"Excellent," said Ms. Vanderpants. "Because the author, Morty C. Mingus, is coming to Stermont Elementary for our 100th Day party. And tomorrow, you're going to help me get ready."

Alexander looked at Stanley's dopey grin. Then he rolled his eyes, rolled up the poster, and got back to work.

CHAPTER 5

EAR WE GO AGAIN

Alexander met Rip and Nikki after school. He pushed his bike so they could walk together.

"We did more experiments on Rip at recess," Nikki told Alexander. "We know one gummy makes his ears turn blue, but if we double it . . ."

She tossed two gummy worms in the air. "Fetch, boy!"

Rip chomped the gummies. His ears became blue and pointy, and a dozen blue freckles bloomed on his cheeks.

"See? The spots are back!" said Nikki. "But he's not fully a monster —"

Rip skidded to a halt. "SHHH!!" he said. "There it is again! Do you hear it?"

"Hear what?" asked Alexander.

"The clicking sound," Rip said.

"Nope," said Nikki. "Sorry, Rip."

"Really?!" Rip said, waving his arms. "It's a bunch of clicks, like dice rolling on a table . . . aw, it's gone again."

"Your ears just faded back to normal, Rip," said Nikki. "Maybe that sound is, like, part of your monster powers."

"Yeah, maybe," said Rip.

They walked a while in silence.

"Oh," said Alexander. "Did your teacher tell you Morty C. Mingus is coming to school for the 100th Day party?"

"The steam shovel writer?" asked Nikki. "Yeah."

"You know, if Ms. Vanderpants invited him, then maybe he's *another* undercover monster," said Alexander. "Like Dr. Tallow!"

Rip snorted. "He MUST be a monster — he created a steam shovel that sings about saying 'excuse me' when you burp!"

Nikki laughed. "Well, I guess we'll keep an eye on him," she said. "There's your house, Salamander. See you tomorrow!"

CHAPTER 6 FEEDING TIME

100th DAY author visit TOMORROW

For the second day in a row, Alexander biked to school super early to snoop around.

Once again, he made his way to the principal's office without being seen.

He was looking behind a bookshelf when he heard footsteps in the hallway. These weren't the tup-tup-tup footsteps of Principal Vanderpants's shoes. They sounded more slappy, like clown feet.

Alexander peeked through a crack in the door. Mr. Hoarsely went tromping by, carrying the steaming bucket.

What's Mr. Hoarsely doing? thought Alexander.

Mr. Hoarsely set the bucket down near the UPSTAIRS BASEMENT door. He looked sweaty. Alexander wondered if it was from the steam, or from fear.

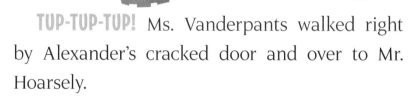

TUP-TUP-TUP! Ms. Vanderpants walked right by Alexander's cracked door and over to Mr. Hoarsely.

"Eep!" Mr. Hoarsely jumped.

"G-g-good morning, Ms. Vanderpants," he said, wringing his hands. "The spaghetti is ready."

"Splendid," said Ms. Vanderpants. "I think it's time *you* started feeding it."

"Do I have to?" Mr. Hoarsely croaked.

Ms. Vanderpants took out a key ring and unlocked the massive door.

RRRUMMMMBBLE! The door to the UPSTAIRS BASEMENT swung open —just a bit. All Alexander could see was darkness.

SCRITCH! The scraping sound was much louder with the heavy door open. It sounded like a garden rake being slowly dragged down a sidewalk.

"EEP!" Mr. Hoarsely's eyes bugged out like a pair of Ping-Pong balls.

"Oh, come on," said Ms. Vanderpants. "You can't be afraid of *every* monster! This beast is nothing like Coach Gill!"

Alexander gasped. *So Principal Vanderpants*

definitely knows about monsters! And she must be keeping one in there!

Mr. Hoarsely looked at his shoes.

"Fine!" said Ms. Vanderpants. "I'll feed it breakfast, but you're feeding it lunch. Today. During recess."

She tossed the keys to Mr. Hoarsely. Then she picked up the bucket, squared her shoulders, and marched into the UPSTAIRS BASEMENT. The door slammed shut.

"Eep!" Mr. Hoarsely ran down the hall, keys jangling with every step.

Alexander swallowed. He was sweating. And it wasn't from the steam.

7 TIGHT SCRAPE

Alexander's brain was spinning as he sat down.

Just play it cool, he thought. *I can't let Ms. Vanderpants know that I know that she knows about monsters! At least, not until I figure out what's in the* UPSTAIRS BASEMENT!

A few minutes later, Ms. Vanderpants staggered into the room.

"Oh. Good morning, Alexander," she said, setting down her now-empty bucket.

Alexander's jaw dropped. He had never seen his principal so . . . messy.

She still had a tightly coiled braid on top of her head, but stray hairs were sticking up. Her sleeve was ripped. And there were long scratches on her hand.

"Ms. Vanderpants!" Alexander said. "What happened?"

She began wrapping a bandage around her scratched-up hand. "I had a . . . breakfast mishap."

She stopped wrapping. Then she took off her glasses and rubbed her eyes.

"Alexander," she said. "This has to end. Now." She looked into Alexander's eyes.

Alexander shivered. Without her glasses, Ms. Vanderpants's eyes seemed dark and cold, like a shark's.

"I've had my eye on you since the day you moved to Stermont," she continued. "I know you've been battling monsters, and —"

RING RING!

Alexander jumped, both from the phone ringing and from the fact that Ms. Vanderpants knew about the S.S.M.P.

"Excuse me," she told Alexander. "This call is important."

Ms. Vanderpants turned to answer the phone, and Alexander's eyes widened.

Jacket ripped to shreds

Strange bumpy vest underneath — armor?

Alexander pretended to read while he listened to the call.

"This is unacceptable," she said into the phone. "I will take care of him myself. My plan can't fall apart now!"

WHAM! She slammed the phone down so hard it cracked.

"Morty C. Mingus is stuck at the airport. I'm going to pick him up," Ms. Vanderpants said. She leaned over Alexander's desk. "We will finish our discussion later. But now, I need your help."

Alexander swallowed.

Ms. Vanderpants gave him a clipboard. "Here are the things I need *you* to do today."

looth Day party tomorrow!
- [ ] blow up balloons
- [ ] decorate auditorium
- [ ] remind school chef to bake 40 dozen steam shovel brownies
- [ ] photocopy programs

Alexander looked at the list, and then up at his principal. She was already heading toward the door. "I hope I can count on you — for everyone's sake."

Principal Vanderpants swept out the door, leaving Alexander alone in the silent office.

CHAPTER 8 SMASHY-SMASHY

Alexander spent the morning crossing things off his to-do list. He finished by copying the programs.

Stermont Elementary
100th DAY PARTY!
With author **Morty C. Mingus,**
creator of Stanley the Steam Shovel!

PROGRAM {
1. WELCOME
2. WORD SHOVELING (How I write.)
3. SNEAK PEEK (Book 83: Stanley ties his shoes.)
4. BROWNIE TIME! (Dig in!)

500

COPY

By the time he made it downstairs, lunch was almost over.

"Salamander!" said Nikki. "Where have you been?"

"Running around," said Alexander. "Listen — I need you both to skip recess. I know how to get into the UPSTAIRS BASEMENT."

Nikki gasped. But Rip was staring off into space.

BRINNGGG!! The recess bell rang. Students began leaving the cafeteria.

Nikki put a hand on Alexander's shoulder. "Whatever you need, Salamander."

Alexander smiled, and then turned to Rip.

Rip blinked. "Huh?! Sorry — those clicks are driving me nuts. WAIT! Skip recess?! Ugh . . . okay, but this had better be worth it."

"Great, let's go!" said Alexander.

The S.S.M.P. double-timed it to the thirteenth floor.

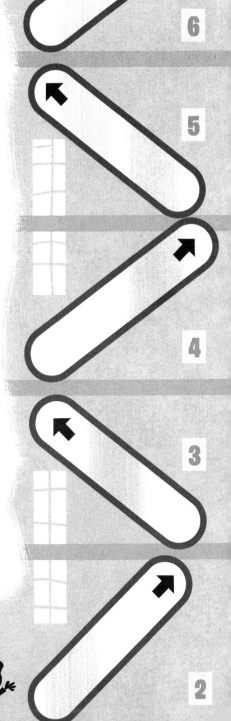

Mr. Hoarsely paced outside the UPSTAIRS BASEMENT, near a steaming bucket of spaghetti.

"Mr. Hoarsely!" Alexander shouted.

"Eep! What are you three doing here?!" Mr. Hoarsely asked. "Ms. Vanderpants isn't going to like this!"

Alexander stepped forward and whispered, "Why don't you let us feed the monster for you?"

Mr. Hoarsely's eyebrows shot up. "You know about . . . *it*?" he asked.

Alexander nodded. "And we know *you* don't want to feed it. Just give us the keys so you can stay out here in this nice, safe hallway."

Mr. Hoarsely's knees began to knock. "No! It's too dangerous! And besides, Ms. Vanderpants would fire me!" He ran down the hall, keys jangling.

"Wait! So what's IT?" Nikki asked Alexander. "Is there a monster in there?"

"The BOSS-monster?" Rip added.

"We won't know until we bust in," Alexander said.

"But how?" asked Nikki. "That door has FIVE locks!"

Rip smiled. "I have an idea, guys." He turned to Nikki. "Hey, jampire. Give me, um . . . eleven gummies."

"No way, Rip! You'll turn into a — ooooohhh! Good idea!" said Nikki. "Here you go!" Nikki tossed him a fistful of gummy worms.

Rip swallowed the gummies.

Monster-Rip lowered his horns and charged at the heavy stone door.

A chunk of the door split off. Monster-Rip fell back to the carpet, dizzy.

Alexander and Nikki watched him gradually shrink back to regular-Rip. He hopped to his feet. "See? More gummies equals more smashy-smashy!" he said.

Cool air rolled out from the opening.

Alexander grabbed the steaming spaghetti bucket, took a deep breath, and led his friends through the dark doorway.

9 SINGLE FILE

The UPSTAIRS BASEMENT was huge, dark, and chilly. It looked like a downstairs basement, except on the thirteenth floor.

Alexander put down the bucket and ran his finger along the wall. There were long, deep gouges scratched into the stone.

GURG-G-GG-GG. A high-pitched growling came from up ahead.

"It's too dark — I can't see," whispered Rip.

"Rip-monsters can't see in the dark, but jampires can!" said Nikki, squinting. "It looks like a machine. It's shiny, and metal. And sharp."

KSSHHHH!!! An explosion of sparks lit up the room. The machine-thing spun toward Alexander, Rip, and Nikki. Sparks flew from where its metal pointy parts scraped the stone floor.

"Look out!" Nikki shouted.

The three friends dove in different directions, leaving the still-steaming bucket near the door. The spinning whirligig tilted left.

"OW!" Rip yelped as part of the spinning thing scraped his boot. He scrambled up the wall, using the deep scratches as toeholds.

SCRITCH-SCRITCH! The metal machine-thing spun in place, like a top.

Alexander's eyes were finally adjusting to the light. The spinning thing stopped. It looked like a silvery metal pig-bear. Its back was covered in hundreds of sharp, poky tines.

The blood drained from Alexander's face. "I know this monster!" he shouted. "It's a forkupine!"

45

FORKUPINE

➤ Metal rodent, covered with forks.

➤ Loves spaghetti.

Rip scratched his head. "The *boss-monster* is a forkupine?" he asked.

"No," said Alexander. "I think this monster's more like a guard dog."

"What's it guarding?" Rip asked.

"That!" said Nikki. She pointed to a metal box in the corner.

"I bet our notebook is in there!" Rip said.

"I remember what forkupines like! I'll lure it away from the box!" said Alexander. He ran toward the bucket.

CLAP-CLAP! "Hey! Poky!" he shouted.

The forkupine spun behind him.

"Nikki!" Alexander shouted. "Kick the bucket!"

Nikki ninja-kicked the bucket. Spaghetti splattered everywhere.

The forkupine zipped over to the wet noodles. The creature twisted and twirled around, smiling.

Alexander dashed over to the box. He opened it. There was no notebook. Just a gray file folder stuffed with lists, maps, and photos.

S.S.M.P.

ALEXANDER BOPP

- Born: Feb. 29
- Leader
- Special one-on-one class with me

RIPLEY BONKOWSKI

- Troublemaker
- Became monster at Putter's Cove mini-golf course

NIKKI HUBBARD

- JAMPIRE!
- Argued with Dr. Tallow almost every day.

DOTTIE ROGERS

- Obsessed wth rabbits
- Attended Camp Gloamy
- Excellent math skills

RETIRED
on 8th birthday

BUMPY
MUM

SHADOW
SMASHERS X

???

OCTO-S

COACH GILL

Fencing instructor
"I never leave home without my sword!"

STERMONT GROCERY
The best-and only-store in town!™

SPAGHETTI   900 BOXES

$1,745.90
TOTAL

Have a pretty good day!

X SNOMBIES

X P-REX

X B. GOONS

X TUNNEL FISH

Hoarsely

X

Z

STERMONT

ADMIT ONE
To see the wonderful, mysterious, amazing
COUNT CHAD!

Alexander slipped the file into his backpack. Then the three friends hurried out, before the forkupine finished slurping its spaghetti.

10 VANDERPLANS

Alexander, Rip, and Nikki flipped through Ms. Vanderpants's secret file on their walk home.

"I can't believe she's been spying on *us*!" said Nikki.

"She must be trying to figure out how to stop us," said Rip. "Look! She even wrote about me turning into a monster at the golf course!"

"This file folder means she's for sure the boss-monster," said Alexander.

"Right," Rip said. "So what kind of monster is she?"

"Good question," said Alexander.

"Well, what kind of powers does she have?" asked Nikki.

"She's strict," said Alexander. "...and she never smiles."

"She's always on time," said Nikki.

"And she, uh, only wears gray," said Rip.

"She was wearing a bumpy leather thing this morning, under her clothes. Sort of like armor," said Alexander.

"You know," said Nikki. "None of these things are really monster powers."

Rip paused and cupped a hand to his ear. "Speaking of monster powers..."

"Do you hear clicking again?" asked Alexander.

"Yeah," said Rip. "But you don't?"

"Nope," said Alexander. "It *must* be related to your monster powers. Can you experiment tonight and practice transforming?"

"You mean eat sugary stuff? Sure!" said Rip.

Nikki twisted her hoodie strings. "I still don't know how we can battle Ms. Vanderpants, when we don't even know what kind of monster she is."

"Whatever she is, we can handle her," said Alexander. "We've been training all year for this! We're quick, and smart, and we have two powerful monsters on our side! You both rest up and meet me in the morning, behind the school. Early."

"For a 100th Day monster battle!" said Nikki.

"Sweet!" said Rip. "Vanderpants won't know what hit her!"

"I'll draw up a battle plan tonight!" added Alexander.

CHAPTER 11 THE COOKIE CRUMBLES

Alexander tiptoed downstairs the next day for an early breakfast. His dad was already there, finishing his *own* bowl of Stanley Flakes.

"Morning, kiddo!"

"Uh, hi, Dad," Alexander said. "What are you doing up so early?"

"Are you kidding?!" his dad asked. "I heard Morty C. Mingus is here in Stermont! I could hardly sleep! I'm taking the day off to come help out at your 100th Day party!"

"Oh," said Alexander. "So . . . I guess I'll see you there." Then he had a quick breakfast and raced to school.

Rip and Nikki were waiting behind the building, as planned.

"So what now, Salamander?" said Nikki.

"We're going to sneak in *there*," Alexander said. He nodded to a door marked STAGE ENTRANCE. "I found this door yesterday when I was decorating the auditorium.

He led Rip and Nikki inside.
They stood in a dark room with
ladders and ropes crisscrossing
above a heavy red curtain.

"We're backstage," said
Alexander. "That means
we've already finished
Step 1 of my super
secret plan." He
pulled a diagram
from his pocket.

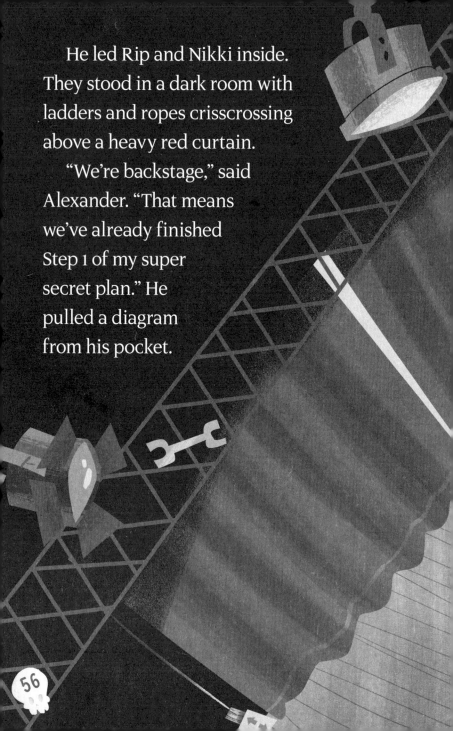

57

SUPER SECRET

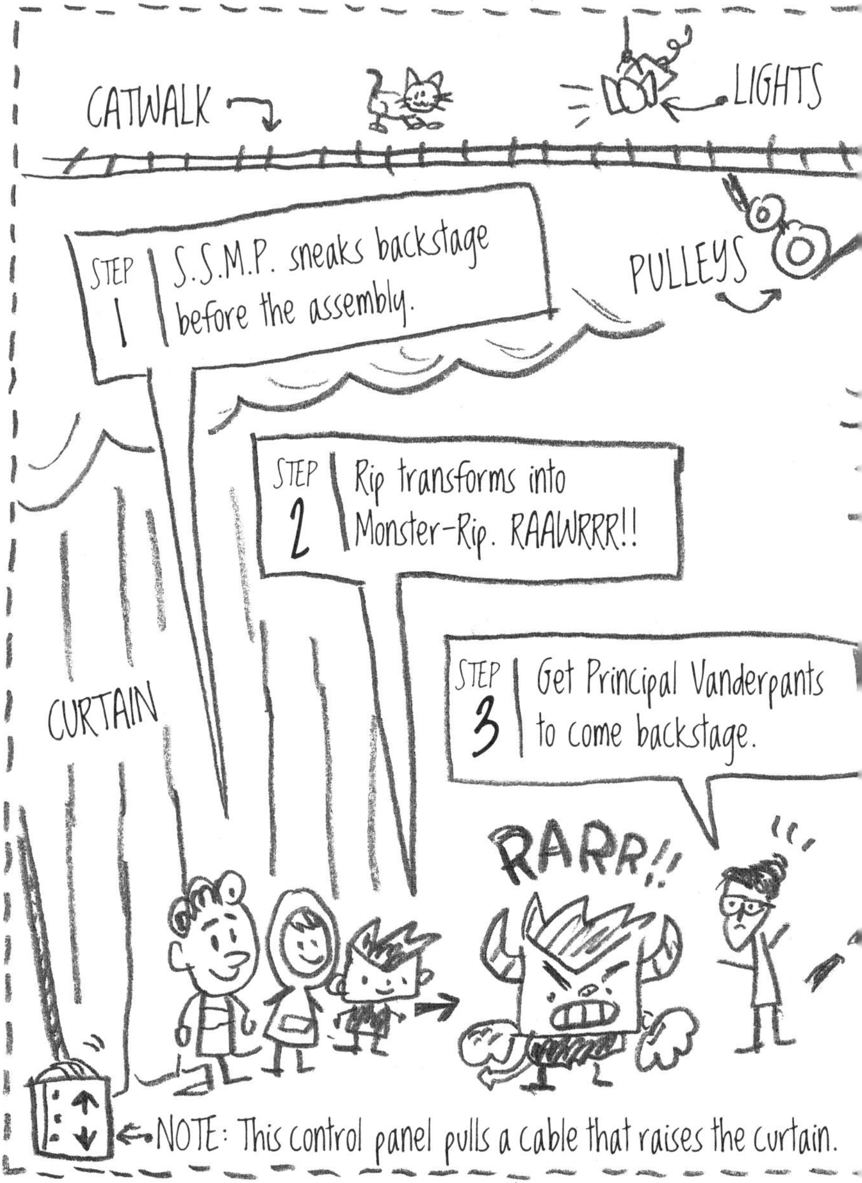

BACKSTAGE PLAN

"Nice plan, Salamander!" said Nikki.

"Thanks," said Alexander. "It should work, as long as Rip can handle Step 2?"

"No problem, weenie!" said Rip, holding up a monstrous cookie. "If I eat this chocolate-chunk-peanut-butter-cinnamon-swirl-butterscotch-fudge cookie, I'll be good to go."

"Awesome!" said Alexander and Nikki.

Rip cocked his head. "I still haven't figured out that clicking sound, though."

"You could try — oh," said Nikki. She brushed an ant off his shoulder. "There. You had another little friend."

"A bunch of little friends," said Alexander, pointing to the ground. "Look!"

A line of ants marched across the wooden floor, right up to Rip's shoes.

"Ack!" said Rip, "They're following me!"

Nikki laughed. "Maybe they want your cookie!"

"Fine, have it!" said Rip. He tossed the cookie to the floor. The ants swarmed in and began nibbling away.

"Oh, shoot!" said Rip. "That was my only cookie!"

"Now how are we supposed to pull off Step 2?" Nikki asked, punching Rip on the arm.

Alexander's shoulders drooped. The assembly hadn't even started, and his plan was crumbling to pieces.

12 STAGE FRIGHT

Alexander peeked through the curtains. The auditorium was filling up fast. Mr. Hoarsely was setting up a microphone. And along one wall was a cafeteria cart, loaded with brownies.

"Ah! Just what we need," Alexander whispered. "Guys, I'll be right back."

"Okay, but hurry!" said Nikki.

Alexander jogged down a dark passageway and through a narrow side door.

He made his way through the crowd. He could see Principal Vanderpants talking to Mr. Mingus, off to one side.

"Ooof!" Alexander bumped into Stanley the Steam Shovel. Actually, it wasn't Stanley. It was someone dressed as Stanley. Actually, it wasn't someone — it was his dad.

"Howdy, Al!" his dad said.

"Uh, hi, Dad," said Alexander. "I can't talk right now — I'm kind of busy."

"Oh, me, too!" said Alexander's dad. "They've got me passing out treats! Here, have a brownie!"

"Thanks, Dad — just what I needed!" said Alexander. He took a brownie and turned to head backstage. But then the lights flashed.

"It's about to start!" said Alexander's dad.

Principal Vanderpants stood onstage.

"Good morning, students," she said, speaking into a microphone. "You know our visiting author from such books as *Stanley Eats His Lima Beans* and *Stanley and the Thank-You-copter.* Let's give a big welcome to Morty C. Mingus."

Mr. Mingus took the stage.

"Thank you, Stermont Elementary," he said. "Why don't I start by telling some knock-knock jokes?"

The crowd clapped politely. Except for Alexander's dad, who was jumping, whistling, and cheering.

Alexander made his way back to the side door.

"WHOA!" said Rip's voice from the other side of the curtains.

Ms. Vanderpants's eyes narrowed as she tilted her head toward the curtains.

Alexander raced along the dark passageway back to his friends.

"Rip," he whispered. "I could hear you out front."

"Sorry, Salamander," said Rip.

"But check out the ants!" said Nikki.

Ants were still swarming around Rip's cookie. But they were no longer black — they were bright blue.

"Whoa!" said Alexander.

"Shhh!" said Rip. "Vanderpants might hear you."

From the other side of the curtain, Alexander could hear the audience groan at one of Mr. Mingus's jokes.

The ants wiggled a bit, and then —

BA-DINK! BA-DINK! BA-DINK!

They grew larger and larger.

The S.S.M.P. was surrounded by an army of huge blue ant creatures.

13 LETTING HER HAIR DOWN

These ants are gi-normous!" said Alexander.

"Gi-norm-ants!" Nikki said.

Bright-blue spots

Clicky antennae

Razor-sharp mandibles

The ants were each about the size of a football. They finished eating the cookie, and then turned toward Rip, antennae wiggling.

An ant nuzzled against Rip's knee. Rip knelt down.

"Careful, Rip!" said Alexander.

"They're not going to hurt us, Salamander," Rip said. "I hear more clicking — it's coming from the ants!"

"They're communicating with you?!" asked Alexander.

"Yeah, I think so!" Rip said, petting a gi-norm-ant. "All these ants remind me of the time that ant farm broke, during our battle with the P-Rex ..."

Nikki's eyes widened. "Rip!" she said. "These *are* those ants! You and the ants ate monster candy that day! Remember?"

"So now you turn into a monster when you eat sweets, and so do they!" said Alexander.

"That's what I was afraid of," said a cold voice. Principal Vanderpants pushed her way through the curtains.

Alexander, Rip, and Nikki all gasped.

"Uh-oh," whispered Alexander. "She wasn't supposed to show up until we were ready for Step 3!"

Principal Vanderpants addressed Alexander, Rip, and Nikki as though she had caught them chewing gum.

"First, you troublemakers let my forkupine escape," Ms. Vanderpants said. She looked at the giant blue ants zigzagging away from her. "And now I've got monster ants to deal with."

"You're the one making trouble!" said Nikki, stepping forward. "We saw your secret file in the UPSTAIRS BASEMENT!"

Ms. Vanderpants paused. Her face turned as red as a gummy worm. "Yes. I've been watching you. But you need to trust me, I —"

"Trust you?!" said Alexander. "The way we trusted Dr. Tallow? The teacher *you* hired — who tried to destroy us? Never! Now where's the notebook? We want it back!"

"Excuse me!" Mr. Mingus's head appeared through the curtains. "Could you keep it down back here? I'm trying to rap about table manners!"

He popped back out.

Alexander gave Rip a look as he wiggled the brownie in his hand. Rip nodded back.

Ms. Vanderpants sighed. "You're totally right, Alexander. If I want you to trust me, I should be honest about who I am."

Then she balled her hands, arched her back, and, with a growl, burst through her gray suit. She had a leathery shell on her back, a long tail, and scaly feet with sharp claws. She pulled a few pins from her hair and uncoiled her braid.

Alexander's jaw dropped. Ms. Vanderpants had a sharp, silvery horn growing out of her head.

"What kind of monster *are* you?" asked Nikki.

"A unicorn-turtle?" said Rip. "A turtle-corn?"

Ms. Vanderpants groaned. "No, Ripley. I'm a nar-madillo. Part narwhal, part armadillo. And now, you three have a choice. You can listen to what I have to say . . . or you're doomed!"

73

CHAPTER 14 BACKSTAGE BRAWL

"**S**tep 2!" Alexander yelled.

He threw the brownie to Rip.

Rip caught it and scarfed it down. In seconds, he was hairy, scaly, toothy, and ready to fight.

GRA-AWW-WRR!!

Ms. Vanderpants hunched down, her tail swinging.

Rip lowered his horns and charged at his principal. She whipped around, blocking Rip's attack with her armored shell.

BLOMP! Rip bounced off her shell and crashed into a stack of stage lights.

"So much for Step 2!" Nikki yelled. She grabbed a broom from a nearby workbench.

Ms. Vanderpants stepped toward Rip, who was still on the ground.

"Leave him alone!" Nikki screamed.

Nikki swung the broom at Ms. Vanderpants's legs, catching her ankles and tripping her to the floor.

But in an instant, Ms. Vanderpants was back on her claws.

"I'm coming, Nikki!" Alexander shouted. He ran for a mop, but tripped over a skittering ant. "Urf!" He crashed into a costume rack, getting his head stuck in a knight's helmet.

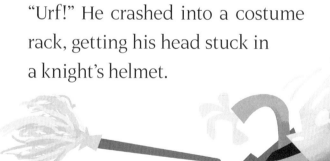

GRAAAWWRR! Monster-Rip roared, and threw a sandbag at Ms. Vanderpants's head. She lunged at the bag, spearing it with her horn. A shower of sand rained down on Nikki.

Nikki staggered, wiping the sand from her eyes, and smashed into Sir Alexander. The two of them bumped into a control panel next to the curtains, and then fell into an oversized drum.

50 POUNDS

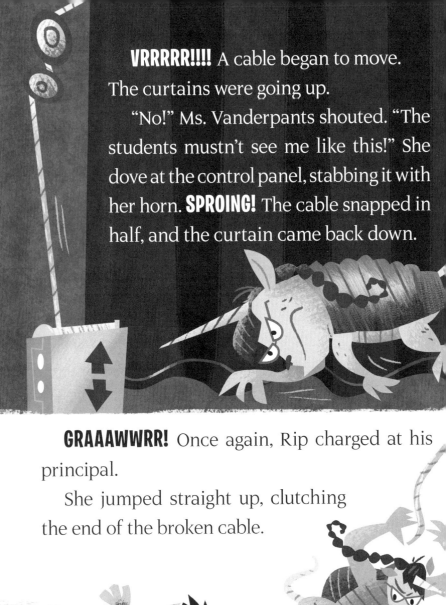

VRRRRR!!!! A cable began to move. The curtains were going up.

"No!" Ms. Vanderpants shouted. "The students mustn't see me like this!" She dove at the control panel, stabbing it with her horn. **SPROING!** The cable snapped in half, and the curtain came back down.

GRAAAWWRR! Once again, Rip charged at his principal.

She jumped straight up, clutching the end of the broken cable.

Rip flew under her. CLONK-KER-BLASH! He plowed into a stack of brass instruments, and fell into the drum with Alexander and Nikki.

"Oof," he said, back in regular-Rip mode.

"Enough," said Ms. Vanderpants. "You *will* listen to what I have to say!"

She held the end of the broken cable in her claws. Then she curled back into a ball and rolled around the S.S.M.P., impossibly fast, tying them to the drum.

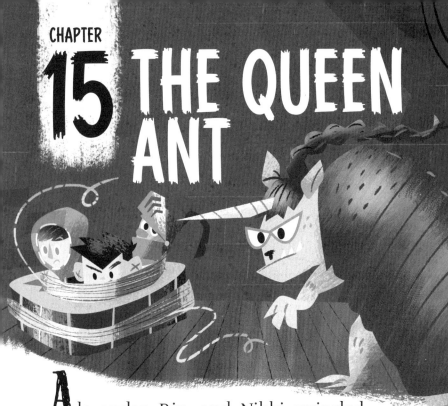

CHAPTER 15
THE QUEEN ANT

$\mathbb{A}$lexander, Rip, and Nikki wriggled against the steel cable holding them in place.

Ms. Vanderpants pointed her narwhal horn at Alexander as she spoke. "Now, Stermont is in serious — Ouch!"

Ms. Vanderpants whirled around. An ant creature had chomped her armadillo tail.

"Shoo, you pest!" yelled
Ms. Vanderpants. She spun
in place, trying to grab the ant.

"The gi-norm-ants!" said
Alexander. "They're trying to
help us!"

More ants skittered toward Rip. They began
chomping at the cable with their sharp mandibles
until — SPROING! — the cable snapped.

Then the ants bowed down to Rip.

"Nice work, guys!" said Rip.

"They must think you're the queen ant! Hurry,
give them an order!" said Nikki, pointing to the
curtains.

"Ants!" said Rip. "Take down those curtains!"

The gi-norm-ants formed a line and marched up the curtains.

They snipped their way across the top of them.

Principal Vanderpants looked up. FLOMP! The curtains crashed down on her.

Morty C. Mingus stopped talking, and turned to look.

Ms. Vanderpants's horn ripped through the fabric. She looked up, seething with anger.

Everyone in the auditorium gasped.

The younger students — and Mr. Hoarsely — screamed and shouted, pointing at Principal Vanderpants and the blue ant creatures. They all scrambled out of their seats, and fled the auditorium.

But the adults and older kids — including Dottie — just seemed surprised that the curtains fell. They didn't seem to notice the monster ants, or that their principal had a horn and a tail.

Mr. Mingus threw up his hands. "As Stanley said in book 38: 'When you run out of steam, shovel off.' I'm out of here!"

He stormed out of the auditorium.

"Wait!" Alexander's dad called, chasing after him. "You forgot to sign my books!"

Ms. Vanderpants untangled herself from the shredded curtain. "You've ruined my plans!" she yelled.

"That's exactly what we wanted to do," said Alexander. "We stopped you and your evil plans!"

Ms. Vanderpants scratched her horn. "Wait. *Evil* plans? What are you talking about? I meant my plans to stop the boss-monster. To get your notebook back."

"Huh?" Alexander said. "But we thought —"

GLAARGHH!!!! A scaly green arm reached down from the catwalk and grabbed Alexander's principal.

"I thought I could count on you, Alexander!" Ms. Vanderpants cried. "But I guess I was wrong..."

The arm pulled her up into the darkness.

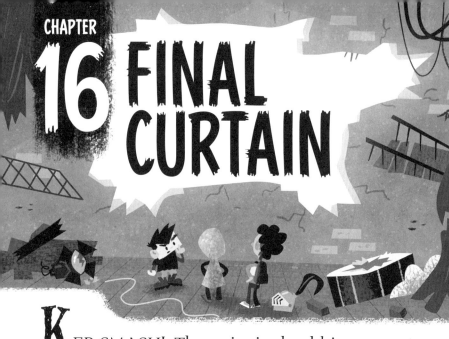

KER-SMASH! The principal-nabbing monster crashed through the back wall of the stage.

Mr. Hoarsely rushed onstage. "Alexander!" he cried. "What have you done?"

"But —" began Alexander.

"We thought —" said Rip.

"She —" added Nikki.

Mr. Hoarsely shook his head. "You trapped the wrong monster! Ms. Vanderpants wasn't the boss-monster!" he said. "She was trying to *stop* the boss-monster!"

Rip looked at the monster-shaped hole in the wall. "You mean, that big ugly green arm —"

"Yes," said Mr. Hoarsely. "Ms. Vanderpants has been trying to defeat the boss-monster for years. And now you just handed her over!"

The S.S.M.P. stood in silence as rubble fell. Rip's ants — back to normal size — crawled up his leg. He no longer tried to brush them off.

"So we still have to find our notebook," said Nikki.

"Yeah," said Alexander. "Just as soon as we save our principal."

Alexander turned over a 100th Day program and sketched some notes about the nar-madillo. Then he handed a program to Rip, to write his own entry.

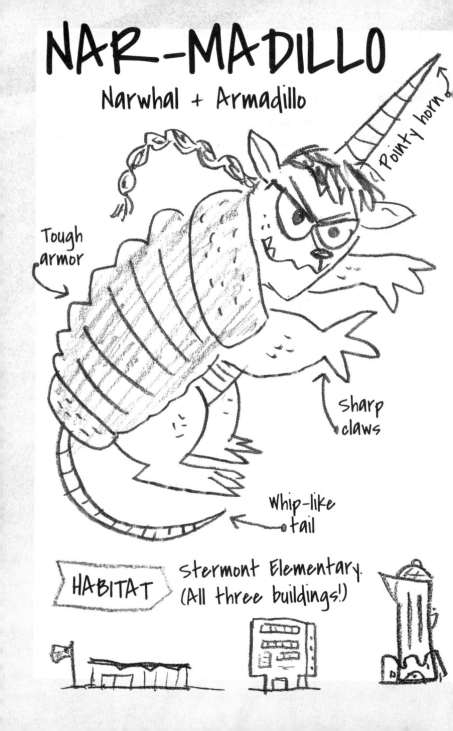

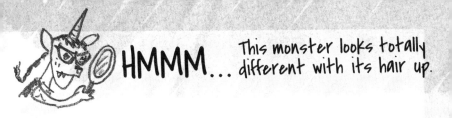

HMMM... This monster looks totally different with its hair up.

The nar-madillo has some powerful monster moves.

BALL SPIN!

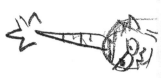

HORN JAB!

SHELL BLOCK!

INCREDIBLE SWIMMER?

WARNING! The nar-madillo doesn't kid around. It's one of the toughest, most serious monsters in Stermont. Try to stay on its good side!

KNUCKLE-FISTED PUNCH SMASHER

So so so so awesome!

HABITAT Awesome places like bike ramps, dodgeball tournaments, and monster truck rallies.

DIET This creature used to eat candy off the ground, but these days he eats mostly cupcakes.

BEHAVIOR This monster is famous for his awesome horns, awesome scales, awesome tail, awesome smashy fists, awesome roar, and handsome eyebrows.

WARNING! Try not to compare yourself to the K.F.P.S. — you'll just end up feeling like a sad, non-awesome weenie.

↳ and don't forget the ⟶

GI-NORM-ANTS!
Super-cool helper monsters

- HUGE SIZE! -

- BRIGHT BLUE! -

CLICKY ANTENNAE

SHARP MANDIBLES!

ARMORED
~~THORX~~
~~THOR AXE~~
~~THRAX?~~
BELLY

TROY CUMMINGS

has no tail, no wings, no fangs, no claws, and only one head. As a kid, he believed that monsters might really exist. Today, he's sure of it.

BEHAVIOR This creature spends most of his time giving assemblies at grade schools. Just like his idol, Morty C. Mingus.

HABITAT Gyms, school libraries, and multi-purpose rooms.

DIET Whatever they're serving at the cafeteria that day. Plus: chocolate milk, of course.

EVIDENCE Few people believe that Troy Cummings is real. The only proof we have is that he supposedly wrote and illustrated The Eensy-Weensy Spider Freaks Out!, and Giddy-up, Daddy!

WARNING Keep your eyes peeled for more danger in The Notebook of Doom #13:

BATTLE OF THE BOSS-MONSTER

THE NOTEBOOK OF DOOM

QUESTIONS & ACTIVITIES!

Reread pages 28 and 29. What does Alexander overhear that makes him certain Principal Vanderpants knows about monsters?

What things are hidden in the UPSTAIRS BASEMENT?

How are Rip and the ants connected? How do the ants help the S.S.M.P.?

How do the adults and older kids react when they see Ms. Vanderpants's true identity? How do the younger kids react?

Look at pages 88-91. Would you rather be a nar-madillo or a knuckle-fisted punch smasher? Write a paragraph explaining your choice.

31901060542984